nickelodeon

IT'S A SPONGEBOB CHRISTMAS!

Don't Be a Jerk—It's CHRISTMAS!

Lyrics by Tom Kenny and Andy Paley • Illustrated by Heather Martinez
Based on the TV series *SpongeBob SquarePants*, created by Stephen Hillenburg, as seen on Nickelodeon

Random House 🏠 New York

created by

Stephen Hillenburg

ISBN 978-0-449-81766-7
randomhouse.com/kids
Printed in the United States of America
10 9 8 7 6 5 4 3 2 1

AHOY, EVERYBODY! SPONGEBOB HERE.

Christmas means
presents and mistletoe,
sharing and caring!

So during this most festive season,
please—don't be a jerk!

Bring joy to the world—it's the thing to do!

But the world does not revolve around you!

DON'T BE A JERK—

IT'S CHRISTMAS!

Be nice to babies and animals,
old folks, too—

'Cause that's how you'd like them to treat you!

Don't screen my calls!

Don't you wreck
the house when you
deck the halls!

Spit your gum where it won't wind up on my shoe!

Squeeze toothpaste
from the bottom
of the tube!

Don't be a jerk—it's Christmas!

When others are talking,
never interrupt!

Don't put people down
or leave the toilet seat up!

It's the time for family
and holly and turkey!

'Tis the season
to be jolly,
not jerky!

Santa brought nearly
every gift on your list. . . .

Why whine about the one that he missed?

DON'T BE A JERK—

IT'S CHRISTMAS!

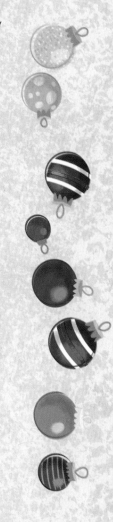

Special Thanks

Kat Beaupre
Mark Caballero
Doug Cohn
Chris Finnegan
Colleen Fitzpatrick
Jennie Hammond
Russell Hicks
Stephen Hillenburg
Pam Kaufman
Boris Kravchenko
Steve Lambe
Sarah Kirshbaum Levy
Rhonda Medina
Jennifer Newfield
Jon Rebell
Elise Rouse
Russ Spina
Claudia Spinelli
Richard Siegmeister
Paul Tibbitt
Katrin van Dam
Seamus Walsh
Stephen Youngwood
Cyma Zarghami
Keith Zurcher
Paula Allen
James Killeen
Drew Podwal
James Salerno